Karen's Big Move

**Other books by
Ann M. Martin**

Leo the Magnificat
Rachel Parker, Kindergarten Show-off
Eleven Kids, One Summer
Ma and Pa Dracula
Yours Turly, Shirley
Ten Kids, No Pets
With You and Without You
Me and Katie (the Pest)
Stage Fright
Inside Out
Bummer Summer

For older readers:

Missing Since Monday
Just a Summer Romance
Slam Book

THE BABY-SITTERS CLUB series
THE BABY-SITTERS CLUB mysteries
THE KIDS IN MS. COLMAN'S CLASS series
BABY-SITTERS LITTLE SISTER series
(see inside book covers for a complete listing)

Little Sister

Karen's Big Move
Ann M. Martin

Illustrations by Susan Tang

A
LITTLE APPLE
PAPERBACK

SCHOLASTIC INC.
New York Toronto London Auckland Sydney

The author gratefully acknowledges
Jan Carr
for her help
with this book.

ISBN 0-590-06594-7

12 11 10 9 8 7 6 5 4 3 2 1   8 9/9 0 1 2 3/0

Printed in the U.S.A.   40
First Scholastic printing, April 1998

Let's Go to Chicago!

Home again, home again. It was my first night back at the little house. I opened my suitcase and took out a sweatshirt.

"Hey, Karen," said Andrew. He walked into my room. Andrew is my little brother. He is four going on five, and he can be a real pain. "I made up a new song," he said. "Do you want to hear it?"

"Not now, Andrew," I said. "I am unpacking."

Andrew did not pay any attention. He started to sing loudly. Actually, it sounded

more like shouting. The words of his song went like this:

"Let's go to Chicago! Chicago! Chicago! Go, go, go, Chicago! Chicago is great!"

I put down my sweatshirt and looked at Andrew. I knew he was worried. My family was planning to move to Chicago for six months, and I had promised Andrew that I would go too. But now I was not so sure. It was a problem. A very big problem.

Maybe I should tell you who I am. My name is Karen Brewer and I am seven years old. I am in the second grade at Stoneybrook Academy. I have blonde hair and blue eyes, and I wear glasses.

Until now, I have always lived in Stoneybrook, Connecticut. Sometimes I live with my mommy in a little house, and sometimes I live with my daddy in a big house. (That is why I could decide not to move to Chicago. I could stay with my daddy at the big house if I wanted. I will tell you all about my two houses soon.)

Mommy came into my room.

"Welcome back, Karen," she said. She gave me a big hug. Then she looked me in the eye. Uh-oh. I was afraid she was going to ask me if I had made my decision yet. But she did not. "Do you have any dirty laundry?" she said instead. "I am just about to put in a load of wash."

Whew! I pulled some dirty socks and a dirty shirt out of my suitcase. I handed them to Mommy.

"Thanks," I said.

Mommy started to leave the room. Then she stopped and turned around.

"Karen," she said, "have you made up your mind yet? Are you going to come to Chicago with us? Or have you decided to stay in Stoneybrook?"

"Well," I said slowly. "I am still thinking."

"Then maybe you should leave out your suitcase. Every time you think of something you might want to take to Chicago, you could put it right in. That way you will not forget anything."

"Good idea," I said. Starting to pack

seemed easy enough to me. It did not mean that I had to go. It just meant I had to *think* about going.

Hmm. What would I need? It was spring, the beginning of April. I might still need a sweatshirt. I laid my sweatshirt back in the suitcase.

Andrew started to dance around in front of me.

"Chicago!" he sang more loudly. "Chicago! Let's go to Chicago!"

"Andrew!" I shouted suddenly. "You are making too much noise! Get out of my room!"

Andrew looked hurt.

"Please," I added. "Please get out of my room."

I guess I was a little upset. It is hard to make such a big decision. I had a lot of thinking to do. And very little time. My little-house family was going to move to Chicago in only two weeks.

I pulled some more things out of my suitcase. Something fell out of my shoe. It was a chocolate that Nannie had made. She must have tucked it into my suitcase as a surprise.

Boo and bullfrogs. I sat down on my bed and sighed. How could I possibly leave Nannie and all the people at the big house? But how could I let my little-house family move without me?

Andrew poked his head back in my door.

"Remember your promise!" he said.

I ran to the door to shoo him away, but my little brother had already disappeared.

Karen, the Expert Mover

I am very good at moving. In fact, I am an expert. Andrew and I move every month. One month we live in the big house, and the next month we live in the little house. I will tell you about the big house and the little house now. There is a lot to tell.

When I was little, I lived with Mommy and Daddy and Andrew in the big house. It was the house Daddy had grown up in. But Mommy and Daddy started to fight a lot. They told us that they loved Andrew and me very much. But they wanted to get a divorce.

Mommy found a little house to move to, and Andrew and I moved with her. Then Mommy met a man named Seth Engle and she got married again. Now Seth is my stepfather and he lives with us in the little house. He brought his dog, Midgie, and his cat, Rocky, with him.

Andrew and I have pets at the little house too. I have a rat named Emily Junior and Andrew has a hermit crab named Bob. That is a lot of people and pets for a little house. But believe me, there are many more at the big house. It is hard to know where to start.

First there is Daddy. Daddy got married again too, and his wife is named Elizabeth. She is my stepmother. Elizabeth already had four children. So now I have three stepbrothers and a stepsister. Sam and Charlie are in high school. (Charlie has a car. Sometimes he drives us places.) Then there is Kristy, who is gigundoly nice. She is thirteen, and the best stepsister ever. And then there is David Michael. He is in second grade, just like me. (He is nice, but I am glad he goes to a different school.)

There are even more people in the big house. I have a little sister named Emily Michelle. Daddy and Elizabeth adopted her from a faraway country called Vietnam. Nannie lives with us too. Nannie is Elizabeth's mother. That makes her my step-grandmother. She helps take care of Emily Michelle. She has just started a business making chocolates. Lucky me! I get to help her. (She lets me eat the ones that do not turn out so well.)

Now I will tell you about the pets at the big house. David Michael has a puppy named Shannon. She is a Bernese mountain dog. Daddy has a cat named Boo-Boo, who is old and fat and cranky. I have a goldfish named Crystal Light the Second, and Andrew has one named Goldfishie. Plus, Andrew and I get to bring Bob and Emily Junior with us wherever we live. As you can see, it is a good thing the big house is *big*.

It is fun to move back and forth, but sometimes it can be confusing. To make things easier, Andrew and I have two of a lot of things, one for each house. We have two sets of clothes, two sets of toys, and two sets of books. I have two bikes, and so does Andrew. (I taught him to ride a two-wheeler.) That way, we only have to pack a few things to bring back and forth. Because we have two of so many things, I made up special names for us. I call us Karen Two-Two and Andrew Two-Two. (I made up the nicknames after my teacher, Ms. Colman, read us a book called *Jacob Two-Two Meets the Hooded Fang*.)

The luckiest part is that I also have two best friends. Nancy Dawes lives next door to the little house and Hannie Papadakis lives across the street and one house down from the big house. We all go to Stoneybrook Academy and we are best friends. In fact, we call ourselves the Three Musketeers.

If I moved to Chicago, I would miss Hannie and Nancy terribly. And how would I pack all the things I needed for six months? I wouldn't have an extra set of clothes and toys waiting for me in Chicago.

If I decided to go, it would be a much harder move than I was used to. And I had to make my decision soon.

Kristy's New Puppy

The next morning, at the bus stop, Nancy was very glad to see me. In fact, she had brought me a treat. She pulled it out of her lunch box.

"I brought you a cookie," she said. "Do you want it now?"

"Thanks," I replied.

Nancy is always nice to me, but suddenly she was being extra-special nice.

When we reached school, Hannie had a surprise for me too. She had made me a card. On the front, she had drawn a picture of the three of us. Inside she had written, "The Three Musketeers Forever! We hope you decide to stay in Stoneybrook. If you leave, we will only be the *Two* Musketeers."

"Gee, thanks," I said. But I was beginning to feel a little funny. What if I decided to go to Chicago? Hannie and Nancy would be very upset.

I did not have time to worry then. Ms. Colman arrived. Ms. Colman is the world's best teacher. She looked at the clock and told us it was time for class to begin. Nancy took attendance. She smiled at me when she called my name.

"Well," said Ms. Colman when Nancy was finished, "I am glad to see that everyone is here today. We are going to start a new unit, and I think you will all enjoy it. We are going to study working animals."

"Goody!" I shouted. (Sometimes I forget to be quiet.)

Ms. Colman looked at me.

"Karen," she said, "do not forget to raise your hand. Since you are so excited about this unit, can you tell us what a working animal is?"

"It is an animal that does work for people," I said.

"That is right," said Ms. Colman. "Can anyone think of some examples?"

I raised my hand right away, but Ms. Colman did not call on me. She called on Addie Sidney instead.

"A sheepdog," said Addie. "They work herding sheep."

Ms. Colman nodded and wrote Addie's answer on the board. I waved my hand, but Ms. Colman looked around the room. She called on Bobby Gianelli.

"Police dogs and fire dogs," he said.

"Two more good answers," said Ms. Colman. I waved my hand harder. I could not wait for Ms. Colman to hear *my* good answer. But she did not call on me. She called on Pamela Harding. Pamela is my best enemy in the class.

"Guide dogs for people who are blind," said Pamela.

14

Oh, no. I slumped in my seat. That was *my* answer. Ms. Colman called on me next, but it was too late.

"I was going to say guide dogs too," I said. "That is a very good answer for me, because soon I will know a lot about them. My stepsister, Kristy, is getting a new puppy. In fact, she is getting her this very afternoon. She is going to take care of the puppy for a year. And then the puppy will go to a special training school and learn to be a guide dog for people who are blind."

"Really?" said Ms. Colman. "That is very interesting."

"Yes," I said. I talked quickly so Ms. Colman would not stop me. "And Kristy told me something very important. People should never pet a guide dog or talk to one when he has his special harness on. The harness means he is working, and he has to stay alert."

"That is a good thing for the class to know, Karen," said Ms. Colman. "I hope you will be able to tell us more about guide dogs as the weeks go on."

"I hope so too," I said.

I did not know if I would be in school in the weeks ahead. I would not be if I moved to Chicago. Then I certainly would not be able to tell the class all the things I knew about guide dogs. My decision was getting more and more complicated.

That afternoon after school, Mommy drove Andrew and me to the big house to meet Kristy's new puppy. As soon as we opened the door, the puppy bounded to us and jumped on me. Kristy came running to get her.

"I see you have met Scout," she said.

Scout licked me with her wet, slobbery tongue.

"You are a very friendly puppy," I told her.

I knew this would help make her an excellent working animal.

Flip a Coin

The next morning on the bus, Nancy acted a little strange.

"Are you still thinking of moving to Chicago?" she asked. "It is very cold there in the winter."

"I will not be there in the winter," I said. "We are only moving for six months."

"Yes, but it is windy all the time," she said.

Nancy and I both know a lot about Chicago. Last month we worked together on a class project about the city. Maybe it was not such a good thing for me that Nancy knew so much.

"The city has a population of three million people," she said. "That is awfully big. You won't know a single person."

"I will know Mommy," I said. "And Seth and Andrew." But suddenly, that did not seem like very many people at all.

At school I found a note on my desk. It said, *Remember. In 1871, Chicago had a big fire. The city burned to the ground. Watch out! This could happen again.*

The note was not signed.

"Look at this," I said to Nancy. Hannie looked at it too.

"Hmm," said Hannie. "Maybe you should think about that. I would not want to move to a city that might have a big fire."

I noticed that Nancy was looking at the floor. Hannie was not looking at me either.

That afternoon after recess, I found another note on my desk. This one read, *BEWARE! A lot of mean gangsters have lived in Chicago.*

I showed the note to Hannie and Nancy.

"Ooh," said Hannie. "Gangsters? Are you sure you want to move to Chicago?"

I was beginning to think I knew who had written the notes. When the school day ended, I waved them in front of Hannie and Nancy.

"Did you write these?" I asked.

"No," they said.

"I think you did. And if you did, it was a very meanie-mo thing to do."

Nancy scuffed her shoe on the floor. "Well," she said, "we did not mean to be meanie-moes."

"Then you did write the notes."

"Yes," Hannie admitted. "But only because we want you to stay."

"Well, it does not help to be mean," I snapped. "It is hard enough for me to make a decision."

I was glad it was Friday. I was hoping I would be able to think more clearly when I got home. But when I walked in the door, Andrew was waiting for me. He had drawn

19

a picture for me. It was a picture of us in Chicago.

"See?" said Andrew. "We are standing on top of a very tall building, waving to all the people. I think we will have fun together in Chicago."

I wished everyone would just leave me alone.

On Saturday morning Mommy took me back to the big house so I could visit Scout. I plopped down on the couch.

"Hi, Karen," said Kristy.

I did not answer.

"What is wrong?" asked Kristy. "You seem awfully quiet."

"I cannot make up my mind," I told her. "I cannot decide if I should move to Chicago or not."

"That is easy," said Kristy. "I will help you. We will flip a coin."

"Flip a coin?" I said. What a terrible idea. "I would not want to do that. Then I would have to do what the coin decides. I want to decide for myself."

"You can," said Kristy. "But the coin can help you. This is the way it will work. Let's say the coin tells you to go. If that makes you happy, then you will know that you *want* to go. If it makes you unhappy, then you will know that you do *not* want to go. You can do exactly as you please. The coin will just help you see how you *feel* about it. It always works for me."

Hmm. Now Kristy's idea sounded like a good one.

"Why not?" I finally agreed.

Kristy pulled a penny out of her pocket. She held it on her thumbnail, ready to flip.

"Heads, you go," she said.

She flipped the coin. She caught it, and slapped it flat on her arm. I peered over to see what the coin had decided.

"Heads," said Kristy. "That means you go. Is that what you want to do?"

I still did not know. The coin had not helped me after all.

"This decision is too, too hard!" I cried.

Ghosts and Goblins

That night, when Mommy tucked me in, she sat down beside me on the bed.

"Karen," she said. "I know you have been trying very hard to make a decision. I wish there was something I could do to help."

"You could tell me what to do," I said. I was only half joking.

Mommy laughed. "You know we are hoping that you decide to come with us," she said. "We will miss you very much if you decide to stay. But I cannot tell you what to do. You have to do what *you* want to do.

22

And I think perhaps you already know what that is."

"That is just the problem," I said. "I do not."

"I mean deep inside," said Mommy. "Somewhere inside you, you already know the answer. The trick is to find out what it is."

Mommy's voice sounded very comforting. But I had no idea what she meant. If I could figure out the answer, there would be no problem.

Mommy kissed me good night and turned off the light. I lay awake in the dark for a very long time. I stared at the shadows on my ceiling. Maybe the answer was somewhere in the shadows.

"Karen?" said a voice. It was Andrew. He was standing in my doorway.

"You are supposed to be asleep," I said.

"I cannot sleep," said Andrew. "There are ghosts in my room."

"Ghosts?"

"And goblins. I think they are hiding in

my closet. And some crawled under my bed. Can I get in bed with you?"

"Okay," I said. I do not always let Andrew get in bed with me. But that night, Andrew looked very scared.

Andrew climbed into my bed. He laid his head on my shoulder.

"Karen, would you sing me a song?" he asked.

"Sure," I answered. "How about 'Old MacDonald Had a Farm'?" Usually Andrew likes that song. He likes to think up unusual animals, such as aardvarks and anteaters.

"Not tonight," said Andrew. "How about the Chicago song?"

I knew what song he meant. He meant the song he had made up about Chicago.

"I do not remember how it goes," I said.

Andrew sang the song for me.

"Now you sing it," he said. He closed his eyes tightly and snuggled deeper into my shoulder.

"Okay." I sighed. I sang the song. "Let's

go to Chicago! Chicago! Chicago! Go, go, go, Chicago! Chicago is great!"

It did not seem to me to be a very good lullaby. But when I looked down, Andrew was already asleep. His hair was sticking up. He was wearing his fireman pajamas. They were all bunched up and wrinkly. Andrew looked very sweet. How could I stay in Stoneybrook and let him go to Chicago without me? What if he got scared at night? I would not be there to sing to him. I realized it was my job to sing to him and take care of him. I was Andrew's big sister.

I knew then what my decision must be. I would go to Chicago. I had promised Andrew that I would go, and that is what I would do. I could not wait to tell everyone in the morning.

6

Karen's Important Announcement

The next morning, I woke up before anyone else. I crawled out of bed without waking Andrew and hurried to the kitchen. It was Sunday. That meant everyone might stay asleep for a very long time. I decided to make myself some breakfast. It would be best to have some food in my stomach when I made my important announcement.

I climbed onto a chair to reach the cabinet where we keep the bowls. I had to stand on my tippy toes. *Bang!* The bowls fell out of the cabinet. They bounced off the counter-top and landed on the floor. Luckily they are plastic.

Then I tried to reach my cereal. Mommy had put the box up high. When I pulled it down, the box tipped over. It rained Krispy Krunchies.

"Karen," said Mommy.

Uh-oh. Mommy was standing in the kitchen doorway. She was still in her pajamas, and she looked cross and grumpy. "What are you doing?"

"What is all that noise?" asked Seth. Oh, no. I had woken up Seth too. Andrew stood behind him, rubbing his eyes. I had woken up the whole family.

I climbed down off the chair. "I am very sorry for waking you all up," I said. "But actually I am glad to see everyone together. I have an announcement to make. And it is important for me to make it to everyone."

"Let me guess," said Seth. "The announcement is that it is time to get up."

"I think we already heard that one," said Mommy.

"Everyone sit down at the table, please," I said, "and I will tell you the news."

Mommy and Seth and Andrew pulled out their chairs and sat down. I stood at the head of the table and clanged a spoon on the sugar bowl to get everyone's attention.

"This meeting is now called to order," I said. "The reason I have gathered you together is because I have some very good news."

"You are going to move to Chicago!" shouted Andrew.

Andrew was ruining my announcement. I clanged my spoon on the sugar bowl once again. "I am going to move to Chicago," I said.

"Yippee!" cried Andrew.

Seth grabbed a dish towel and tossed it high in the air.

"This calls for a special breakfast!" he said. "How about strawberry waffles?"

Mommy leaned over and gave me a kiss.

"Great news, honey," she said. "We are very glad. I think I'll celebrate with a cup of coffee."

Seth got busy making waffles, and Mommy measured coffee into the coffee filter. I picked up the phone.

"Who are you calling, Karen?" asked Mommy.

"I am calling the big house," I said. "I need to tell them my important news too."

"Well, you cannot call them now," said Mommy. "Everyone there is probably still asleep. You will have to wait at least an hour."

"An hour!" I cried. That did not seem fair. "What will I do for an hour?"

"You can start by cleaning up the mess you made," said Mommy.

"Oh," I said. It was going to be a very long hour.

Finally it was time to call the big house. Daddy answered the phone.

"Daddy," I said, "I have something to tell you. I have decided what I will do. I am going to move to Chicago with Mommy and Seth and Andrew."

At first Daddy did not answer. "I am sorry to hear that," he said at last. "You know that we will miss you very much."

"I will miss you very much too," I said. "That is why it was so hard for me to make my decision. But I will be back in six months."

"Karen," said Daddy, "I am glad you finally figured out what you want to do. But if you change your mind for any reason, do not forget what we decided. You can always come back to the big house. Your mom and I do not want you to be unhappy."

"Thank you, Daddy," I said.

Suddenly my eyes were teary. Sometimes knowing that so many people love me makes me cry.

The Two Musketeers

I did not tell Hannie and Nancy my decision on Sunday. I decided to wait until I saw them together at school the next day. I knew they would not be happy with my news.

"I have something to tell you," I said to Nancy when I reached the bus stop.

"You do?" she asked. She looked worried.

"Yes," I said, "but I want to tell you and Hannie together. So I will wait until we get to school."

"Karen!" cried Nancy. "That is not fair! You have to tell me now."

"I will tell you when we get to school," I said firmly.

The bus pulled up to our stop. Nancy and I found a seat in the front. Nancy pestered me all the way to school.

"You have decided to move, haven't you?" she asked. "You are going to Chicago. I know it."

"Maybe. Maybe not," I said.

"Karen, you cannot go. You will hate it there. You will not be with your friends. It will be terrible."

"It will not! I will be with Mommy and Seth and Andrew. And it will only be for six months."

Oops. I had spilled the news. The bus pulled into the driveway of our school. Nancy ran into our classroom ahead of me. When I came in, she was already talking to Hannie.

"Guess what," she blurted out. "Karen is moving to Chicago."

"Karen, you cannot!" cried Hannie. "You cannot leave just two Musketeers!"

The other kids gathered around us. Every-one started talking at once, pushing closer to me to ask questions. I could not hear what anyone was saying. Ms. Colman came into the room.

"Well," she said, "it looks as if something exciting has happened."

"Karen is moving to Chicago after all," said Nancy.

"My," said Ms. Colman. "That *is* news. That will certainly be a big change for you, Karen."

It was time for class to start. We took our seats. Then Ms. Colman told us that she had a surprise for us. It was part of our unit on working animals.

"We are going to read *Black Beauty*," she said. "It is a very beautiful and sad book about a horse who had many hard jobs. In the book, Black Beauty tells his story in his own words. Because some of the language is a bit hard for second-graders, I will read it to you. I will read some of it each day until

the start of spring vacation. And then we will finish it when we return."

Black Beauty sounded like a gigundoly wonderful book. I could not wait for Ms. Colman to start it. But I realized I would not be able to hear the whole story. I would be in school for only one more week. Friday would be the last day of school before spring vacation. And on Saturday my family would move.

Ms. Colman picked up the book. Before she started to read, she asked us some questions.

"How do you think humans should treat animals?" she asked.

I remembered to raise my hand. Ms. Colman called on me.

"People should treat animals with kindness," I said. "That is why Kristy took in the puppy who is going to be a guide dog. She wants to give her lots of love so she gets used to people."

"That sounds like a very good idea," said Ms. Colman.

36

"I was hoping that Kristy could bring Scout to class," I continued. "Then you could meet her, and Kristy could tell us all about guide dogs. But now there will not be time. My family is moving very soon."

"It must feel a little sad to be moving," said Ms. Colman.

"Sad *and* happy," I said. But suddenly I did not feel too happy.

"Our class will be very different without you," said Ms. Colman. "We will all miss you, Karen."

Then she opened the book and started to read.

"The first place that I can well remember was a large pleasant meadow with a pond of clear water in it."

I loved the story already. I was sorry I would not be in class to hear Ms. Colman read the end of it.

Miles and Miles of Piles

I knew it would be hard to pack, but I did not realize *how* hard. I would have to bring along every single thing I would need.

As Mommy had suggested, I left my suitcase open and put things in as I thought of them. My suitcase filled up quickly. Then I stacked things in a pile on the floor. The pile got tall very fast. I started a new pile. Soon I had lots of piles. I stacked them up along the walls of my bedroom. There were so many things I would need!

"Karen," said Mommy when she saw the piles. "What is all this? Your room is a mess."

"These are the things I will need," I explained.

"Oh, honey," said Mommy, "you cannot take so much. We are not hiring a big moving van. We are only renting a small trailer to hitch to the back of our car."

"But I need these things," I said.

Mommy picked my ice skates off the top of one of the piles.

"We will be coming back in the fall," she said. "You can leave your ice skates here and use them next winter."

"But what if we go to an ice rink?" I asked.

"Then we will rent skates," said Mommy. She picked up something else. "What is this?" she asked. "Your desk lamp? Why did you put that on the pile?"

"How will I see to do my homework?" I said.

"Karen, we are moving to an apartment that already has furniture in it. We do not need to bring things like lamps."

"Oh," I said.

"And what are these?" asked Mommy.

"Books."

"These are picture books you read when you were younger."

"But maybe Andrew will want to read them," I said.

"Karen," Mommy said firmly. "We cannot take all of these things. You have miles and miles of piles here. You must choose a few things to bring and put the rest back."

Boo and bullfrogs.

Just then the phone rang. Mommy answered it. When she came back to my room, she looked happy.

"Well," she said, "that is settled. We have found someone who wants to live in our house while we are gone."

"What?" I cried. "Somebody is going to live in our house?"

"Yes," said Mommy. "Just as we will stay in someone else's home in Chicago, someone *else* will stay in our house here. It is a family who lives nearby. Their house is being fixed up and repaired. So they need another place to stay in while the work is being done."

"A family!" I cried. "You mean they have children? You mean somebody else is going to stay in my room?"

"Yes," said Mommy. "I think they have a girl your age."

This was very bad news. Somebody else was going to be sleeping in my bed, sitting at my desk, going through my closets and my drawers.

"Well," said Mommy. She started to leave. "You have quite a job to do here. You need to put most of these things away. Better get started now."

Mommy was right. I would have to

start immediately. I had to sort through the piles, but that was not all. If some other girl was going to stay in my room, I would have to hide my precious belongings.

Karen Helps Nannie

Soon we would move. Soon I would leave my big-house family for six whole months. I wanted to see them a lot before we left. Mommy said I could visit the big house one afternoon after school. I rode the bus home with Hannie and ran right in the front door.

"I'm here!" I shouted. No one answered. That is very unusual for the big house. So many people live in it. Someone is always around.

I found Nannie in the pantry off the

kitchen. She was making chocolates. She had a big order to fill.

"Who is this for?" I asked.

"Some party," she said. "I can never keep all my orders straight. But it is a good thing you came along, Karen. You can help me."

Nannie opened the cabinet and took out a new mold. It was a big one, shaped like a flower.

"What do you think of this?" she asked.

"Cool," I said.

Nannie tested the temperature of the chocolate that was cooling in a bowl. I sat on the tall stool to help stir.

"Nannie," I asked, "have you ever been to Chicago?"

"Not since I was a spring chicken," she said. "But I remember liking it. Better pack a windbreaker. They call Chicago the Windy City."

"What if I do not like it?" I asked. "What if I miss everyone here at the big house too much?"

"Well, you know you can come back," said Nannie. "Just like your father told you."

The front door banged open. It was Kristy. She peered into the pantry. Scout was with her on a leash. She tugged toward me and sniffed.

"Hi, Karen," said Kristy. "Sorry I cannot stay to talk to you. I have to baby-sit this afternoon. Got to run!"

Kristy pulled Scout out of the pantry. The front door banged open again. This time it was Sam and Charlie. They stopped in the pantry too. Sam was tossing a baseball.

"Hey!" cried Nannie. "No balls inside! This is my work space, not a baseball diamond."

Sam grinned. "Sorry, Nannie." He tossed the ball to Charlie. They ran upstairs. Nannie shook her head.

"Those boys are worse than the puppies," she said. "Every time I see them, their feet get bigger. Their sneakers take up half the floor."

46

David Michael ran into the pantry.

"Nannie, Nannie!" he cried. "Sam and Charlie are playing ball in the house!"

Daddy heard David Michael shouting and came out of his study. "What is going on?" he asked.

"Well," said Daddy when David Michael had told him. "It is a good thing we have a policeman in the house. Just tell the boys to take the ball outside. Tell them I said so."

David Michael ran upstairs. Daddy returned to his study.

Soon Emily came into the kitchen. "Candy!" she shouted. She reached for the mold. "I want candy!"

"Sorry," said Nannie. "No candy now."

Emily threw herself onto the floor and kicked and screamed.

"She did not have her nap," Nannie explained.

"Do you see why I will miss the big house?" I asked her. "There is always so much going on here. I will even miss Emily Michelle's tantrums."

Nannie laughed. I stirred the chocolate, then helped Nannie pour it into the mold. I knew it was going to be hard to be away from my big-house family. Six months was going to seem like a very long time.

Surprise!

Before I knew it, it was Friday. That was the last day of school before vacation, and the day before my move. When I woke up, I had a funny feeling in my stomach. I did not want to say good-bye to all my friends.

When I arrived at school, I stopped to put my books on my desk. Nancy ran to join the other kids. They were huddled together in a corner of the room, and they were whispering. When I joined them, they grew very quiet. Some even started to walk away.

"Well," I said loudly. "That is very rude." I had not even moved, and already my friends had forgotten about me.

At lunch and recess, everyone acted strange. On the playground, Hannie and Nancy whispered with Addie and Natalie.

"Are you telling secrets?" I asked. "You are acting like meanie-moes. Especially since I am moving tomorrow. I would think you would be nice to me."

But after recess, I got a big surprise. When I entered our classroom, I saw Kristy standing with Ms. Colman. Scout was with her!

"Look who has come to visit our class, Karen," said Ms. Colman. "Kristy is going to talk to us about guide dogs for the blind."

I looked at Hannie and Nancy. They were grinning. So that is what all the whispering had been about!

Kristy gave a very good talk. She told us about the puppy program for guide dogs.

She told us that it is good for the puppies to be raised in families instead of kennels. That way, they can get used to a lot of people. They also get used to different places and other animals.

"I will take her to a special obedience class on weekends," she said. "Then, when she is twelve or fourteen months old, she will be old enough to go back to the school for guide dogs and begin her special training."

After Kristy's talk, Ms. Colman quieted the class.

"It is almost time to end the day," she said with a twinkle in her eye. "But first, I think we all have something to say to Karen. One, two, three . . ."

"Surprise!" everyone yelled.

Yikes! My class had a good-bye party for me, with cake and cookies and juice. I was glad to find out that my friends loved me after all. Ricky Torres even made a speech.

"Karen," he said, "we will all miss you. You are a very funny person and you have lots of good ideas for our class. We hope you have fun in Chicago."

I would really miss Ricky. He is my pretend husband. I probably would not get another pretend husband when I moved to Chicago.

Then my friends gave me cards they had made. Even Pamela had made one. It said, "2 sweet 2 B 4-got-10."

"Thanks, Pamela," I said.

All these surprises made it harder for me to say good-bye when the school day finally came to an end. It was hardest of all to say good-bye to Ms. Colman. I gave her a great big hug.

"You are the best teacher in the whole wide world," I said. "I bet there is no teacher in Chicago anywhere as good."

"Oh, Karen," said Ms. Colman, "I do hope you like your teacher there. I bet he or she will be lots of fun and have lots of interesting projects."

"What if I do not like my teacher?" I asked. Suddenly my eyes got teary. "What if

I miss everyone in Stoneybrook?" I knew Daddy had said I could come back. Even so, moving seemed scary.

Ms. Colman gave me a gentle hug.

"It is hard to leave the people you love," she said. "But you will meet lots of new, interesting people."

Hannie and Nancy were standing close by.

"Don't worry," said Hannie. "We will send you E-mail every day."

E-mail. That was a good idea. And Seth had said there would be a computer I could use when we got to our new house in Chicago.

"We will E-mail you twice a day on weekends," Nancy promised. "We will tell you everything that is going on. It will almost be like you are here."

Kristy and Scout were waiting for me at the door.

"Karen," called Kristy, "are you ready? Charlie is waiting for us outside in his car."

"I guess I am," I said. It was time for me to go to the big house. I had more good-byes to say there.

I waved good-bye to Ms. Colman. "See you sometime next fall," I said.

More Good-byes

Charlie drove Kristy and me to the big house. I sat in the back of the car with Scout.

"I will miss you, girl," I whispered in her ear.

When we pulled into the driveway, I saw that Mommy and Andrew had already arrived. Andrew ran toward me.

"Karen!" he cried. "Seth picked up the trailer for the back of the car. It makes a really cool noise when you jump in it."

"Seth is at home packing up the trailer," Mommy told me.

Once again I got that funny feeling in my stomach. We were really leaving. And it was time to say good-bye to my big-house family.

Kristy opened the door and we walked inside. The big house seemed quiet — too quiet. Maybe Nannie was in the pantry, making her chocolates. Maybe Sam and David Michael were still at school.

"Anybody home?" called Charlie. No one answered. Charlie headed for the kitchen. Kristy and Scout did too. Mommy and Andrew and I stood alone in the center of the living room. Mommy shrugged.

"I guess we will have to wait until everyone comes home," she said. She sat down on the couch.

We did not have to wait long. Suddenly everyone in my big-house family ran into the living room.

"Surprise!" they called.

Another surprise! Elizabeth carried in plates of food and set them on the tables. Nannie carried in a plate of chocolates. In the center was the big one shaped like a flower, the chocolate we had made a few days before.

"Is this the party you were talking about?" I asked. "The one you said you could not remember?"

"This is the party," she replied with a wink.

Just then Hannie and Nancy arrived. More kids from the neighborhood showed up too. Someone handed me a cup of juice. Someone else handed me some chips.

Kristy set a pile of presents on the coffee table.

"You have a lot of loot here, Karen and Andrew," she said. "You better start opening them, or we will be here all night."

Everyone gathered around as Andrew and I opened our presents. There were round, squashy packages from Sam and Charlie. Inside were baseball caps.

"Chicago Cubs caps," Sam pointed out. "You will not be able to see *our* games this summer, but maybe you will see a Cubs game."

"All right!" said Andrew. He clapped the cap on his head.

Kristy had picked presents especially for Chicago too. She got Andrew a kite and me a set of wind chimes.

"Because you are moving to the Windy City," she said.

Everyone was so thoughtful. I started to cry. Mommy handed me a napkin to wipe off my glasses.

Just then Scout jumped up on the table and grabbed a slice of ham in her mouth.

"Hey!" shouted Kristy. She ran after Scout. Sam and Charlie ran too. Everyone started to laugh. I looked at my big-house family, at Daddy and Elizabeth, at Nannie and Emily Michelle and David Michael. They were all laughing, but I was feeling sad. It was hard to say good-bye.

Andrew was watching me. He took my hand.

"You and I can fly the kite," he said. "We will have fun in Chicago. Really we will."

I hoped Andrew was right.

Good-bye, Stoneybrook!

The next day, I woke up bright and early. It was Saturday, moving day. I still had something to do before we left, something important.

I got out my markers and a fresh piece of paper and sat down at my desk. At the top of the paper, I drew a skull and crossbones (the scary picture that is on a pirate flag). At the bottom I wrote, "Keep away. This means you!"

It was a very good sign. I put tape on the back and stuck it on the drawer of my dresser. That is where I had hidden all my prized possessions. I did not want some strange girl ruining my things.

After that, I got dressed and looked for Andrew. He was in his room, saying good-bye to his own things.

"Good-bye, bed," I heard him say. "Good-bye, lamp. Good-bye, closet."

Out the window, I could see Seth in the driveway. He was strapping our bikes to the rack on top of the car. Mommy came into Andrew's room. She had jobs for us to do.

"Karen," she said, "could you please strip all the sheets off the beds? And Andrew, I have packed some snacks for the car. Could you please take them out to Seth?"

I pulled the sheets off Andrew's bed. When I went back in my room, I looked at the sign I had hung on my dresser. Hmm. The skull and crossbones looked a little meanie-mo-ish. Maybe the sign was not really a good idea. Maybe it would even make the girl who was staying in my room *want* to look in the dresser. I took down the sign and crumpled it up. Mommy came in the room with clean sheets.

"Well," she said as she stretched the sheets over my mattress, "time to go."

"Really?" I gulped.

"I'm afraid so," she said. She smoothed the hair off my forehead. "It is going to be a good move, Karen," she said. "You will see. You are moving with your family. We will all be going together."

Mommy took my hand and we joined Seth and Andrew. I started to climb into the car. Just then, Nancy ran out of her house in her pajamas to say good-bye.

"Oh, Nancy," I said. I hugged her hard. "We are really moving."

"Come back soon," she said. She was crying. I started to cry too. "And don't forget," she said. "Watch out for gangsters." We laughed and cried at the same time.

I climbed into the backseat of the car with Andrew. (Rocky and Midgie and Bob and Emily Junior were caged up behind us.) Seth started the engine.

"Good-bye, Nancy!" I called.

"Good-bye, little house," said Andrew. "Good-bye, driveway. Good-bye, trees."

I kept my eye on our house as we drove down the street. When Seth turned a corner, I could not see it anymore.

"Good-bye, Stoneybrook," I said.

We were on our way.

Hello, Chicago!

It took us a long time to drive to Chicago. Andrew and I played a lot of car games. (My favorite was license plates. I spotted license plates from forty of the fifty states!)

By the time we reached Chicago, it was Sunday afternoon. We drove past lots of tall buildings. Andrew pointed to the tallest one of all.

"Is that where we are going to live?" he asked.

Seth laughed. "No," he said. "That is the Sears Tower, the tallest building in the city.

In fact, it is the tallest in the whole country. The buildings you see here are mostly office buildings. We will live in a different part of the city."

Seth drove us to a neighborhood where the buildings were a little smaller. He parked the car on the street.

"We are going to live *here*?" I asked. The buildings still looked awfully big to me. They were much bigger than the big house.

Seth pointed to some windows that were very high. I counted up. The windows were on the fifth floor.

"That is our apartment," said Seth.

"Where is the yard?" asked Andrew.

"There is no yard," said Mommy. "When you live in a city, you do not always have a yard."

"Then where will I fly my kite?"

"We can walk to the lake," said Mommy. "And we will go to the parks."

Andrew and I helped Mommy and Seth unload the trailer. We carried the boxes into the lobby of the building. Then we rode the elevator up to our floor. When Seth unlocked the door to our apartment, I peered inside. The living room was very big.

"Wow!" said Andrew.

I ran ahead to look at the bedrooms. One bedroom had a lot of toy cars lined up on a shelf, and a bedspread with dinosaurs on it. That would definitely be Andrew's room. Next to that was a room with a frilly, pink canopy bed. I flopped down on the mattress. I had never slept in a bed with a canopy before.

Someone had left a note on the pillow.

"Welcome to Chicago," it said. "I hope you like staying in my room. Make yourself at home and have fun. Your friend, Jillian."

Hmm. Maybe I should have left a note like that in my room. I was glad I had at least torn up the sign with the skull and crossbones on it.

"Karen!" Mommy called me from the living room. She needed my help moving more boxes.

The four of us spent the rest of the afternoon unpacking. By dinnertime we were very hungry.

"There are some restaurants near here," said Seth. "We could take a break and get a bite to eat. It might be fun to go for a walk in our new neighborhood."

The restaurants were on a street with a lot of stores. The people I saw did not look exactly like the people in Stoneybrook. Our waitress had a green streak in her hair. Andrew stared at her while she took our order.

"Your hair is green," he said.

"Is it?" she said. She patted the top of her head. "I always forget. Last week it was blue."

"Wow," said Andrew.

After dinner, we went into a bookstore. Mommy bought me a map of Chicago. After she had paid for it, we unfolded it.

"Our house is right here," she said, pointing to a spot on the map.

By the time we returned to our apartment, I was very tired. Mommy and Seth stayed up to do some more unpacking. But Andrew and I got ready for bed.

"Can I hang up my wind chimes before I go to sleep?" I asked.

"Maybe we should hang them inside your room," said Seth. "That way, they will not disturb the neighbors. We can open the window so the wind comes in."

Finally I was settled in the big canopy bed. Andrew knocked on the wall between our rooms. I knocked back.

"Good night," I called out.

I could hear people walking around in the apartment above ours. From below, I heard music playing loudly on a stereo. A breeze rustled my wind chimes. A siren screamed by. Chicago certainly was a lot noisier than Stoneybrook.

At last I fell asleep.

Seeing the Sights

The next morning when I woke up, I was not sure where I was. The wind chimes tinkled in the breeze. The ruffles fluttered on my canopy. Oh, yes. I was in Chicago, in my new room. I walked to the kitchen. Mommy was fiddling with the buttons on the coffeepot.

"I wonder how this thing works," she said.

Seth came in the front door of the apartment. He was carrying a bag of bagels he had bought at a deli nearby.

"Breakfast!" he called.

I took a bagel with lots of things on it.

"That is called an everything bagel," said Seth. "It has poppy seeds, sesame seeds, onion, salt, and more."

Yum. I hoped we would have bagels every morning.

That day we still had lots of unpacking left, but Mommy had a good idea.

"I think we should do some sightseeing," she said. "We can do a little bit every day. Seth does not have to start work until Friday, and Karen does not have to start school until next Monday."

"What about me?" asked Andrew.

"You will start preschool the week after," said Mommy.

"Then I want to go to that tall building today," said Andrew.

"I think that can be arranged," said Seth. "There are a lot of fun places to visit in the Loop."

"The Loop?" I asked.

"That is what they call the area downtown," said Seth.

I was glad we were going to go sightseeing. That sounded like fun.

Seth was right about the Loop. We rode the el train to get there. We had to climb up a tall flight of stairs to reach the track. (Mommy explained that it is called the el train because it is *el*evated, which means it is very high above the ground.)

When we got downtown, we went first to a building called the Water Tower. Inside were lots of stores. There was also a waterfall! We rode in glass elevators up to a big department store called Marshall Field's.

"Cool," said Andrew. "This is like a rocket ship!"

Mommy let me buy a sweater in Marshall Field's. It had blue and green stripes.

"Just like our waitress's hair," said Andrew.

After the Water Tower, we took a bus to the Sears Tower. We rode in another elevator to get to the top. It was such a long ride that my ears popped! On the top floor was an observatory. The people on the streets looked like ants, and the cars looked like toy cars. Then Andrew and I took turns looking out a telescope at the city below.

Before we headed home, we stopped to buy hot dogs at a little store next to the el station.

"These are called red hots," said Seth. "Chicago is famous for them."

Red hots were very good. Andrew and I each ate two.

On the ride home I took out the sweater I had bought at Marshall Field's. Mommy pointed out the window.

"Oh, look, Karen," she said. "Can you see that redbrick building over there?"

"Yes," I said.

"That is your school."

My school? The building did not look like a school to me. It was big — much bigger than Stoneybrook Academy.

I put the sweater back in the bag and hugged it to me. I could not wait to get back

to our apartment. I wanted to E-mail Hannie and Nancy. I wanted to tell them about the big school I would be going to.

The train rumbled noisily on the track.

"Here is our stop," said Seth.

I followed him out of the train. I wished I could still go to Stoneybrook Academy. Why did everything in Chicago have to be so *big*?

Museum Fun

The rest of the week was a little bit like a vacation. Mommy and Seth and Andrew and I had a lot of work to do around our new house. But we also did a lot more sight-seeing. One morning Mommy told us we were going to the museums. Andrew was not sure this was going to be fun.

"Museums?" he said. "Do they have red hots at the museums?"

But the museums turned out to be very interesting. First we went to one called the

Art Institute of Chicago. Outside the front door were two big stone lions.

Inside, we saw an Egyptian tomb.

"Spooky," said Andrew.

We walked past a mummy. I grabbed the back of Andrew's neck and said, "Boo!" Andrew screamed and swatted at my hand.

"Karen," he said when he realized it was me. "That was not funny at all."

After that we went to the Museum of Science and Industry. That was really cool. We saw a coal mine. (Well, it was not a real mine. It was an exhibit built to look like a mine.) We even got to go down a mine-shaft.

"Wow," said Andrew. "It is really dark in here."

My favorite exhibit was a fairy-tale castle, with tall turrets and lots of rooms with tiny dollhouse furniture inside. I saw a miniature bearskin rug and a gold grandfather clock that really worked. The castle even had a library with a little dictionary and shelves and shelves of tiny books.

"Bor-ing," said Andrew. "Can we have red hots now?"

"So, what do you think?" Mommy asked as we left. "Do you like Chicago?"

"It has good museums," I admitted. I wanted to go back to the apartment. (I still did not like to call it home.) I wanted to E-mail Hannie and Nancy and tell them about the fairy-tale castle. Maybe some-day they could visit me in Chicago. Maybe I could show them all the things I had seen.

As soon as we returned, I checked my E-mail. Letters were waiting for me from both Hannie and Nancy. I read Hannie's first.

"Dear Karen," it said. "Today I saw Kristy. She was outside walking Scout. She is such a pretty dog. And so friendly. She licked my face and got slobber all over my best jacket."

Scout licked Hannie's face? That was not

78

fair. Scout was *my* dog. At least, she was in my family.

Suddenly the things I had done in Chicago did not seem very interesting. Suddenly I just wanted to go home.

Bikes and Balls

The week sped by. On Thursday morning we took a bike ride along Lake Michigan. The lake was only a short ride from our house. A bike path ran alongside it.

"Look!" cried Andrew. "Kites!"

On the beach, people were flying kites in the strong Chicago wind.

"Karen," said Andrew, "you and I could come here and fly *my* new kite."

"Maybe," I said. I did not want to say yes. Actually, I did not want to do anything more in Chicago. I had begun to hope that I could leave. But I did not say anything about this to anyone. I did not know how.

Andrew and Seth and Mommy pedaled ahead on the path. I pedaled slowly. Mommy fell back to join me.

"Karen," she asked, "are you okay? Usually you ride so fast."

"It is hard to pedal in this wind," I said. "Can I go back now? You could all go on without me."

"I am sorry," said Mommy, "but I cannot let you go back by yourself. Chicago is a big city. You cannot go outside without an adult."

"Boo and bullfrogs," I said.

"Soon we will stop for a picnic," said Mommy. "I packed deviled eggs, just for you."

"I am not hungry at all," I said.

Mommy was quiet for awhile as she pedaled beside me. "Maybe you are feeling homesick," she said. "Maybe it is because we are not very busy this week. Once you start going to your new school, you will not have as much time to think about things."

I wished Mommy had not brought up the subject of my new school. Suddenly I felt much worse.

"Come on," said Mommy. "How about catching up with Seth and Andrew? They will wonder what happened to us."

I pedaled harder, to please Mommy. But I was not having fun on the bike ride. I did not *want* to have any fun. Not in Chicago.

That afternoon, we went to a baseball game at Wrigley Field. Andrew and I wore the Cubs caps that Sam and Charlie had given us. It was a close game. The Cubs won. Andrew cheered and cheered.

"Did you like the game, Karen?" Seth asked me on the way out of the stadium.

"It was all right," I said.

Mommy and Seth looked at each other. I could tell they were beginning to worry about me. That was fine with me. I hoped they did worry. Maybe if they were worried enough, they would even decide to send me home.

As soon as we got back to the apartment, I checked my E-mail. I had not received anything from Hannie or Nancy that day. And nothing from my big-house family either. It seemed as if everyone had forgotten about me already. I sat down to write some letters. Mommy poked her head into my room.

"Who are you writing to?" she asked.

"The big house," I said.

"Oh. You can tell Sam and Charlie about the Cubs game."

"No, I need to ask Kristy about Scout. I need to ask her how her obedience class went."

Mommy watched me for a long time. Finally she left me alone. After I sent E-mail to Kristy, I wrote letters to Hannie and Nancy. Soon it was time for bed. I went into the bathroom to brush my teeth. Andrew was already at the sink. He was still wearing his Cubs cap with his pajamas.

"That was a cool game, huh?" he said.

"If you like baseball," I answered. I spit my toothpaste into the sink. Then I went to my room and climbed into my bed. Andrew knocked on the wall between our bedrooms. He liked to do that every night now, before we went to sleep.

"Good night," he called to me.

"Good night," I called back. I stared at the big pink canopy hanging over the bed. I did not like that canopy anymore. I just wanted to be back in my own big-house bed.

A Long Morning

On Friday, Seth started work. That left Andrew and Mommy and me alone in the apartment. Mommy did not plan any sightseeing trips for us that day. When I woke up, she was already busy in the kitchen.

"I think I will make a big pot of soup," she said. "That way, I can put some in the freezer. Would you like to help me, Karen?"

"No, thank you," I said. I poured myself a bowl of cereal and went back to the computer. There was still no mail for me. I decided to write some more letters. Andrew appeared in the doorway.

"Hey, Karen," he said, "maybe we could fly my kite today."

"We cannot go to the lake without an adult," I replied.

Andrew ran into the kitchen to talk to Mommy. Then he ran back to me.

"Mommy said she might be able to take us to the lake this afternoon," he said.

"I think I am busy this afternoon."

"Busy?"

"I have a lot of letters to write," I said.

"Well, when are we going to fly my kite, then?" asked Andrew.

"Maybe never." I knew I was being a meanie-mo. But I was not feeling very well. In fact, I was starting to feel sick. I did not understand why my friends in Stoneybrook had not sent me any more E-mail. They had promised to write every day. I checked my mail again.

Finally! There was a letter from Nancy.

"Karen," asked Andrew, "do you want to play el train with me? We could make the train out of blocks. We could make a tall track too."

I turned around and looked at Andrew. I did not know I was going to shout, but that is what I did.

"Can't you see that I am busy?" I yelled. "Please do not ask me to play anymore. I have a lot to do."

Andrew backed out of the room. I did not mean to hurt his feelings, but I wanted him to leave me alone. When he had left, I read Nancy's letter.

Dear Karen, it said. *Vacation is fun, but I cannot wait for Monday. I miss school! I hope Ms. Colman reads us another chapter of* Black Beauty *right away. Are you going to finish reading the book by yourself? I love learning about working animals. It is soooo interesting.*

I turned off the computer and walked into the kitchen.

"Mommy," I said, "I want to go back to that bookstore. I need to buy a copy of *Black Beauty*."

"We cannot go right now," said Mommy. "I am in the middle of making soup, and that will take at least a couple of hours. I will take you to the bookstore this afternoon. How does that sound?"

"I guess it will have to be okay," I muttered.

Andrew tugged at my sleeve.

"And after the bookstore we could go to the lake to fly my kite. Right?" he asked.

I yanked my sleeve out of his hands.

"I do not want to fly your stupid kite," I said. I stomped back to the computer and plopped myself down in front of the blank screen.

Oh, boy. It was going to be a long morning.

Then it was going to be a long day.

And then it would be a long weekend.

But most of all, it was going to be a *very* long six months.

A Very Bad Stomachache

On Saturday, I still did not feel well. By Sunday, I felt really sick. I lay on the couch in the living room. I did not change out of my pajamas the entire day. Andrew brought his cars into the living room to play close by.

"I guess you do not feel like flying my kite with me today, do you?" he asked.

"I guess not," I said.

Mommy took my temperature. She shook down the thermometer and put it under my tongue.

"You do not have a fever," she told me. "What exactly feels wrong?"

I held my stomach and groaned. "My stomach," I said. "It feels terrible, really terrible."

Mommy brought me some chicken soup and let me eat it on the couch. Andrew watched me closely.

The next morning I did not feel any better. Mommy came into my room to wake me for school.

"I feel much worse," I said.

"That means you will miss your first day at your new school," she said.

"Oh." I tried to sound disappointed.

Mommy put her hand to my forehead. She looked at me worriedly. Finally she agreed to let me stay home.

That morning I wrote E-mail letters to Hannie and Nancy and my big-house family. In the afternoon, Mommy told me she would read a chapter of *Black Beauty* to me. She fluffed up the pillows on my canopy bed and sat down. I settled back into her arm as she read from the copy of the book I had bought.

"Karen," Mommy said when she finished the chapter, "you seem unhappy lately. Is something bothering you?"

I thought about telling Mommy the truth. I thought about telling her that I did not want to stay in Chicago, that I wanted to go back to Stoneybrook. But what if she got angry? What if her feelings were hurt?

Andrew came into the room and climbed on the bed with us. I knew I could not talk to Mommy in front of Andrew. Andrew would be very upset if I did not stay in Chicago. I was his sister. And I had promised I would stay. If I left, he would be all alone with Mommy and Seth.

"Nothing is the matter," I said. "I am just sick."

"Well, I hope you feel better tomorrow," said Mommy. "I think you will be happier when you are busy at school."

I did not think so at all. I never, ever

wanted to go to that school. I would stay sick until June if I had to.

That night, when it was time for bed, Andrew knocked on the wall between our rooms to say good night. This time I did not knock back. Andrew appeared in my doorway.

"Good night, Karen," he said.

I put my pillow over my head. I did not want to see Andrew or talk to him. I listened to the sound of his footsteps as he walked back to his room.

After that, I lay in bed for a long time. I listened to the tinkling of my wind chimes and to the clanging, banging noises in our apartment building. When I was sure that Andrew was asleep, I got out of bed. I walked into the living room to talk to Mommy and Seth.

"Mommy, Seth," I said, "I have to talk to you. I have something important to say."

"Yes?" said Mommy. "What is it, Karen?" She took Seth's hand.

"I do not want to stay in Chicago," I said.

Mommy and Seth listened for a long time as I told them how unhappy I was.

"Daddy said I could come back to the big house if I wanted to," I said. "Do you think I could go back? Please?"

"We know you have been unhappy," said Mommy. "But if you go back, you cannot change your mind again. You would have to stay at the big house until we return in the fall."

"Does that mean I can go?" I asked.

Mommy sighed. "We will miss you very much," she said. "But we want to do what is best for you. So, yes, you can go."

That was very good news. I would have to call Daddy right away and tell him.

But how would I ever tell Andrew?

19

A Talk with Andrew

The next morning when I woke up, I felt a lot better. I hopped out of bed. Andrew was already in the kitchen, eating his cereal.

"Hey, Karen," he said, "you do not look sick anymore. Is your stomachache better?"

"Much," I said.

"Are you going to get ready for school now?"

I looked at Mommy.

"I am not going to school today," I said carefully.

"Then maybe we can fly my kite."

"I think that might be a good idea," said Mommy. "The three of us could walk down to the lake. You two could fly the kite together." Mommy winked at me. I knew she meant that that would be a good time for me to tell Andrew my news.

After breakfast we walked to the lake. It was a clear, sunny spring day. The wind at the lake was just right for kite flying. Mommy sat on a bench and read a book while I helped Andrew get his kite in the air. I handed him the ball of string. Then I put my hand on my little brother's head. I was not sure how to begin.

"Andrew," I said, "remember when I promised you that I would come to Chicago with you and Mommy and Seth?"

"Yes," he said, "and I am very glad you came."

I sighed. "Well, I think it was a mistake for me to move this time."

"Oh no it was not," Andrew said quickly. "We are all together. We are having a lot of fun in Chicago."

"I am not having any fun," I said. "And I think it would be much better for me to go back to Stoneybrook." I took a deep breath. I looked Andrew in the eye. "In fact, I have decided to go back."

In the sky, the kite was jumping wildly in the wind. Andrew's eyes welled up with tears.

"No," he said. "I do not want you to go back."

"I have already called Daddy," I said. "I am going to leave in a few days."

Andrew dropped the kite string. I grabbed it up quickly. He threw his arms around my waist.

"I will miss you," he said.

"I will miss you too. But we can talk to each other on the phone, and I can send you E-mail letters."

"But who will knock-knock on the wall with me when it is time for bed?" Andrew asked. Tears ran down his cheeks. He was sniffing hard.

"Maybe I can knock on my wall at the big

house, and you can knock on your wall here," I said. "And somehow we will know that we are knock-knocking good night to each other." That gave me another idea. "I know!" I said. "We can send each other knock-knock jokes. I will send you one every night at bedtime. You love knock-knock jokes. Hey, let's make up some right now."

Andrew and I sat down on the bench. Andrew wiped his tears with his sleeve.

"You make one up first," I said.

"Okay." Andrew thought for a moment. "Knock knock," he began.

"Who is there?" I asked.

"Andrew."

"Andrew who?"

"Andrew Brewer!"

That was not very funny, but it was Andrew's idea of a knock-knock joke. Mommy put her arm around Andrew then.

"Did Karen tell you her news?" she asked.

Andrew nodded.

"You know," she said, "you and I and

Seth will have each other while we are in Chicago. And Karen will join us as soon as we move back to Stoneybrook."

It had grown very windy, too windy to stay at the lake. We pulled in the kite and headed back to the apartment.

I felt sorry to be leaving Andrew and Mommy and Seth, but I was very glad I would be going home. I still had to E-mail Hannie and Nancy and tell them my news. They would be so surprised!

Home, Sweet Home

My last days in Chicago went by very fast. Before I knew it I was on a plane heading back to Connecticut. Daddy picked me up at the airport and drove me to the big house. He pulled my suitcase out of the trunk and carried it up to my room. I carried Emily Junior's cage.

"I'm home!" I cried as I walked through the front door. Elizabeth poked her head out of the kitchen.

"Hey, Karen," she called. "Welcome back. I am so glad to see you."

Nannie rushed through the room. She stopped when she saw me and gave me a big hug.

"Karen," she said, "you are back! That is wonderful. Excuse me, please. I have to check on my chocolates."

Just then Scout bounded into the room. Shannon ran in behind her. The puppies rolled around together on the floor. Kristy came in with Scout's leash.

"Time for your walk," she was saying. "Karen!" she cried when she saw me. She threw her arms around me and lifted me high. "It is great to have you back."

Kristy hooked Scout to her leash and headed outside. When she opened the door, Sam and Charlie burst in. They were tossing a baseball back and forth, playing keepaway from David Michael.

"Hey," said David Michael. "Give me back my ball. You know the rule. No balls in the house."

Sam tossed the ball back to David Michael. He ran past me and pulled my ponytail.

"Hey, Karen," called Charlie, "glad to be home?"

He did not wait for an answer. He followed Sam up the stairs. Emily Michelle slid down the stairs past them on her belly. She ran toward me, her arms held wide. Elizabeth picked up Emily.

"Glad to see Karen?" she asked. "Well, give her a kiss hello."

Emily Michelle smacked at the air.

"Good girl," said Elizabeth. "Now it is time for your bath."

Emily Michelle wiggled to get free as Elizabeth carried her off. I grinned. It certainly was busy in the big house.

"Home, sweet home," I said.

I carried Emily Junior upstairs to my room. I had more unpacking to do. But first I would E-mail my family in Chicago and tell them I had arrived safe and sound. I had a special message for Andrew. It was a knock-knock joke I had thought up on the plane. I wrote out both his part and mine so

Andrew would know exactly how the joke went.

"Knock knock," I wrote.

"Who is there?"

"Shirley."

"Shirley who?"

"Shirley you must know that I miss you. Hope you come home to Stoneybrook very soon!"

About the Author

ANN M. MARTIN lives in New York City and loves animals, especially cats. She has two cats of her own, Gussie and Woody.

Other books by Ann M. Martin that you might enjoy are *Stage Fright*; *Me and Katie (the Pest)*; and the books in *The Baby-sitters Club* series.

Ann likes ice cream and *I Love Lucy*. And she has her own little sister, whose name is Jane.

Little Sister

Don't miss #97

KAREN'S PAPER ROUTE

"Karen, do *not* fall asleep!" said Kristy.

"Sorry," I replied. I shook myself awake and folded some more. When we finished, there was a little pile of papers in front of me and a big stack in front of Kristy.

"Next time, you fold them all," Kristy said. "Folding was supposed to be your job."

It was time to deliver. I thought that would be the fun part. But my legs were not cooperating. I felt as if I had jelly knees. They hardly held me up. I watched Scout race out of the house. I wondered where she got her energy. I wished she could give a little of it to me.

LITTLE APPLE™

B·A·B·Y·S·I·T·T·E·R·S™
Little Sister

by Ann M. Martin,
author of The Baby-sitters Club ®

☐	MQ44300-3	#1	Karen's Witch	$2.95
☐	MQ44258-9	#5	Karen's School Picture	$2.95
☐	MQ43651-1	#10	Karen's Grandmothers	$2.95
☐	MQ43645-7	#15	Karen's In Love	$2.95
☐	MQ44823-4	#20	Karen's Carnival	$2.95
☐	MQ44831-5	#25	Karen's Pen Pal	$2.95
☐	MQ45645-8	#30	Karen's Kittens	$2.95
☐	MQ45652-0	#35	Karen's Doll Hospital	$2.95
☐	MQ47040-X	#40	Karen's Newspaper	$2.95
☐	MQ47044-2	#45	Karen's Twin	$2.95
☐	MQ47048-5	#50	Karen's Lucky Penny	$2.95
☐	MQ48230-0	#55	Karen's Magician	$2.95
☐	MQ48305-6	#60	Karen's Pony	$2.95
☐	MQ25998-9	#65	Karen's Toys	$2.95
☐	MQ26280-7	#70	Karen's Grandad	$2.95
☐	MQ69183-X	#75	Karen's County Fair	$2.95
☐	MQ69188-0	#80	Karen's Christmas Tree	$2.99
☐	MQ69193-7	#85	Karen's Treasure	$2.99
☐	MQ69194-5	#86	Karen's Telephone Trouble	$3.50
☐	MQ06585-8	#87	Karen's Pony Camp	$3.50
☐	MQ06586-6	#88	Karen's Puppet Show	$3.50
☐	MQ06587-4	#89	Karen's Unicorn	$3.50
☐	MQ06588-2	#90	Karen's Haunted House	$3.50
☐	MQ06589-0	#91	Karen's Pilgrim	$3.50
☐	MQ55407-7	BSLS Jump Rope Rhymes		$5.99
☐	MQ73914-X	BSLS Playground Games		$5.99
☐	MQ89735-7	BSLS Photo Scrapbook Book and Camera Package		$9.99

- -

Available wherever you buy books, or use this order form.

Scholastic Inc., P.O. Box 7502, 2931 E. McCarty Street, Jefferson City, MO 65102

Please send me the books I have checked above. I am enclosing $ _____
(please add $2.00 to cover shipping and handling). Send check or money order – no
cash or C.O.Ds please.

Name _____ Birthdate _____

Address _____

City _____ State/Zip _____

Please allow four to six weeks for delivery. Offer good in U.S.A. only. Sorry, mail orders are not
available to residents to Canada. Prices subject to change.

BLSG497